Level 3

Branch

KU-327-957

words
stories

Princess
and the Pea

Stories adapted by Shirley Jackson
Illustrated by Roger Langton
Series designed by Jeannette Slater

Copyright © 2000 Egmont World Limited, a division of Egmont Holding Limited.
All rights reserved.
Published in Great Britain by Egmont World Limited, Deanway Technology Centre,
Wilmslow Road, Handforth, Cheshire SK9 3FB
Printed in Germany
ISBN 0 7498 4662 3
A CIP catalogue record for this book is available from the British Library

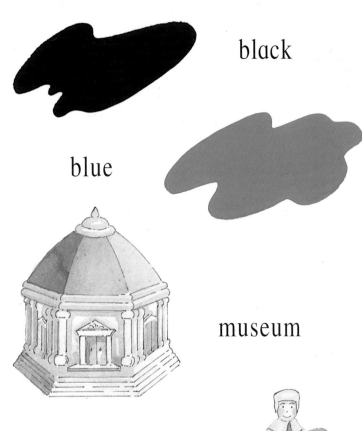

black

blue

museum

servants

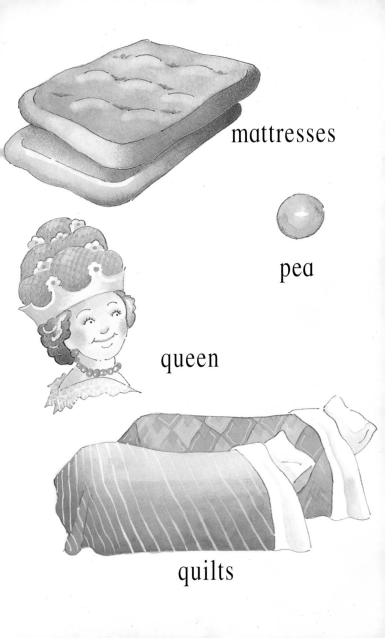

mattresses

pea

queen

quilts

Once upon a time there was
a handsome prince.

The prince was looking for
a wife.

He looked all through
the land.

new words **there** **wife**

His wife had to be a princess.

She had to be beautiful, good and kind – she had to be a real princess.

The queen had an idea.

new words **be** **kind** **idea**

On a cold, black, wet night,
there was a knock at the door
of the castle.

Servants ran to the door.

There was a beautiful girl.
She was blue with cold.
She looked very tired.

new words **wet** **night** **knock** **tired**

"Please let me in," said the beautiful girl. "I am wet and and cold and tired. Do you have a bed for the night?"

"Come in, come in," said the queen.

new word **Please**

The prince and girl talked and
talked and talked.

When the girl went to bed,
the prince said, "I want to
marry that girl."

new words   **talked**

"We must see if she is a real
princess," said the queen.

"We must see if she is good
and kind. I have an idea."

new words **must** **see**

The queen called for the
servants.

"Please make a bed for
the girl," she said.
"Put twenty four quilts on top
of twenty four mattresses."

ew words **called** **put** **twenty four** **top**

When the bed was made,
the queen put a pea under the
twenty four quilts and
twenty four mattresses.

"Only a real princess will
feel the pea. She will not
sleep at all," said the queen.

new words **under** **only** **feel**

The girl had some food.
Then she went to bed.

The girl climbed on top of
the twenty four quilts and
twenty four mattresses

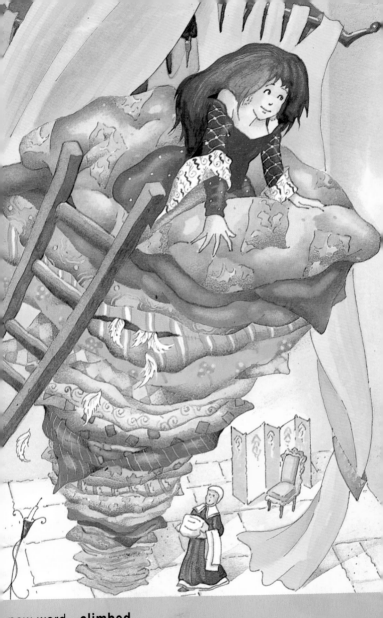

new word **climbed**

In the morning, the girl
climbed down.

She looked very tired.

"Good morning," called the
queen. "You do look tired.
Did you have a good night?"

"No," said the girl. "I did not sleep at all. I could feel something in my bed. I am black and blue all over."

new word **over**

The queen was very happy.

"You must be a real princess," she said. "I put a pea under the twenty four quilts and twenty four mattresses. Only a real princess will feel that!"

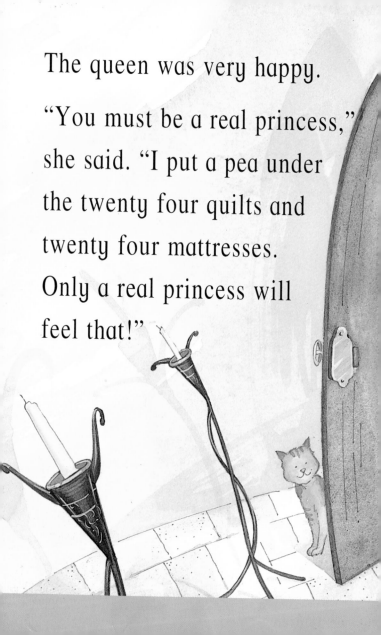

no new words

The prince married the girl.

They lived happily ever after.

And the pea was put in
a museum!